Whose Bottom?

Written by **Fiona Munro**
Illustrated by **John Haslam**
Designed by **Nicola Theobald**

Ladybird

Can you guess who I am?
I'm much **bigger** than you.
The size of my bottom
should give you a clue!

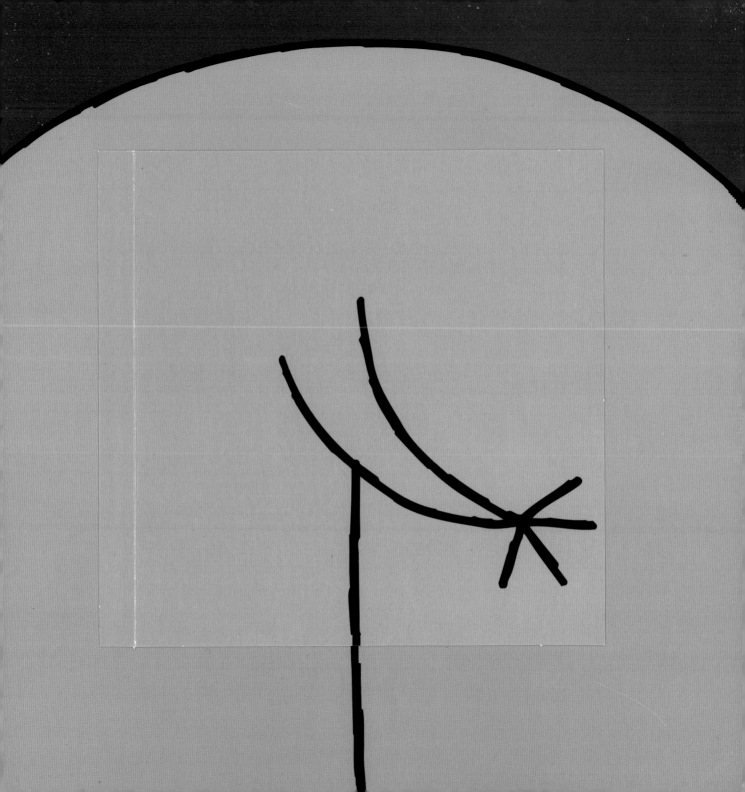

Who am I? Do you know?
I'm hard to spot in
the ice and snow.

My bottom is fluffy and I frolic all day.
Can you guess who I am –
are you coming to play?

It's beautiful here in the snow and ice,
although I can't fly, swimming is nice.

We all love our bottoms,
and hope you do too.
Wouldn't our bottoms look funny on you!